Ivy

To my sisters
Susan, Nan and Kate
and my brother Tim
with love from the favorite

ISBN 0-439-07771-0

Copyright © 1998 by Laura McGee Kvasnosky. All rights reserved.
Published by Scholastic Inc., 555 Broadway, New York, NY 10012,
by arrangement with Candlewick Press.
SCHOLASTIC and associated logos are trademarks and/or registered
trademarks of Scholastic Inc.

12 11 10 9 8 7 6 5 4 3 2 1   9/9 0 1 2 3 4/0

Printed in the U.S.A.   14

First Scholastic printing, March 1999

This book was typeset in Myriad Tilt.
The pictures were done in gouache resist.

Zelda and Ivy

Laura McGee Kvasnosky

SCHOLASTIC INC.
New York   Toronto   London   Auckland   Sydney
Mexico City   New Delhi   Hong Kong

Chapter One

CIRCUS ACT

"Let's play circus," said Zelda.
"You can be the fabulous fox on the
flying trapeze."

"Okay," said Ivy. She put on a fancy
hat and sat down on the swing.

"I'm the oldest," said Zelda. "I will
announce your tricks."

Zelda stepped to one side. She held
out her baton.

"Behold," she said, "the Fabulous
Ivy on the Flying Trapeze."

Ivy started to swing back and forth.
She pointed her toes. She flipped her tail.
She smiled a big smile.

"And now," said Zelda, "the fabulous Ivy
will stand on the flying trapeze." Ivy carefully
stood up. She kept swinging back and forth.

"And now," said Zelda, "the fabulous Ivy will stand on one paw."

Ivy stood on one paw. The swing wobbled.

"Holding on with only one paw," added Zelda.
Ivy tried to hold on with only one paw. She
tried to keep smiling.

"And now," said Zelda, "the fabulous
Ivy will perform a death-defying trick:

balancing on the tip of her tail!"

Ivy fell off the swing. She started to cry.
"Don't worry," said Zelda as she helped
her little sister dust off. "I have trouble with
that trick, too."

Chapter Two

THE LATEST STYLE

"Let's doozy up our tails like movie stars,"
said Zelda.

"I like my tail the way it is," said Ivy.

"It will be even more beautiful with
a blue stripe," said Zelda. She reached
for the paint.

"Do you really think so?" asked Ivy.
She turned to see her tail in the mirror.

Zelda painted a bright blue stripe down Ivy's tail.

"The stripe brings out your natural highlights," said Zelda.

"Oh my," said Ivy, "I'm not so sure."

"Relax," said Zelda. "Stripes are cool."

"Shall I paint a stripe on your tail?" asked Ivy.

"Wait until I'm done," said Zelda. "I'm going to make your tail even better with scallops."

"Scallops?" said Ivy. "I don't know anyone who has scallops."

Zelda cut scallops into Ivy's fluffy tail.
"Oh dear," said Ivy, trying to smooth her tail fur.
"Don't worry," said Zelda. "Scallops are glamorous."
"Shall I scallop your tail?" asked Ivy.

"Wait until I'm done," said Zelda. "Here's the
final touch." Zelda sprinkled golden glitter up
and down Ivy's tail.

"Oh my," said Ivy, shaking her tail.

Zelda picked up her baton. She stepped back and pointed at Ivy. "Voilà!" she said. "A masterpiece!"

Ivy looked down. "I kind of liked it better plain," she said.

"Plain is okay," said Zelda, "but this look is the latest style."

The sisters stood side by side in front of the mirror. Ivy's tail dripped paint and glitter and tufts of cut fur. Zelda's tail was fluffy and red.

Ivy picked up the scissors.

"Shall I doozy up your tail like a movie star now?" she asked.

Zelda quickly swished her tail away.

"Maybe some other time," she said. "Let's take a bubble bath."

Chapter Three

FAIRY DUST

Ivy sat on the front porch and drew stars on the screen door with her blue crayon. Zelda marched around the yard, twirling her baton.

"May I have a turn with your baton?" asked Ivy.

"Not now," said Zelda. "It's still too new for me to share."

Zelda twirled her way up the steps. She watched as Ivy colored in a very large star. Little bits of crayon piled up on the porch below the star.

"Look at this," said Zelda, picking
up the crayon bits. "Magic fairy dust."
 "Really?" asked Ivy.
 "Oh yes," said Zelda, twitching her
whiskers. "If you put this under your
pillow and dream of your wish, it will
come true."

Zelda marched and twirled her way
back down the steps. Ivy carefully
gathered the magic fairy dust.

That night Ivy put the fairy dust under her pillow.

"I wish for a baton," she said.

"It might not work the first time," said Zelda.

"A silver baton with red ribbons on the ends, just like yours," said Ivy.

"It probably lost its magic during the day," said Zelda.

"I will dream of marching and twirling just like you," said Ivy. And she went to sleep.

But Zelda could not sleep. She looked at
her baton shining in the moonlight on the
chair. She listened to the soft snores of her
sister sleeping below her in the bunk bed.

Finally, she hopped down and quietly put
her baton next to Ivy's pillow.

In the morning when Zelda woke up, Ivy was already marching around, twirling the baton.

"Look, Zelda," she said, "my wish came true! I have a baton exactly like yours."

"Yes," said Zelda, a little sadly, "exactly like mine."

"I'm going to twirl and march all day," said Ivy. "Get your baton and twirl with me!"

"Oh," said Zelda. "My baton . . ."

"I'll get it for you," said Ivy. "You left it on the chair last night."

Ivy looked
on the chair.

She looked
under the chair.

She looked
behind the chair.

Then she looked closely
at the baton in her hand.

"I see," Ivy said slowly. She brushed the red ribbons against her chin.

"Zelda," she offered, "we can share my baton together."

"Thanks," said Zelda. "I am the oldest, so I will go first."

Zelda